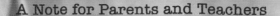

A Note for Parents and Teachers

A focus on phonics helps beginning readers gain skill and confidence with reading. Each story in the Bright Owl Books series highlights one vowel sound—for *Greedy Beetle,* it's the long "e" sound. At the end of the book, you'll find two Story Starters, just for fun. Story Starters are open-ended questions that can be used as a jumping-off place for conversation, storytelling, and imaginative writing.

At Kane Press, we believe the most important part of any reading program is the shared experience of a good story. We hope you'll enjoy *Greedy Beetle* with a child you love!

For all bright-eyed, bright owl readers.

long e

Library of Congress Cataloging-in-Publication Data
Names: Coxe, Molly, author, illustrator.
Title: Greedy Beetle / by Molly Coxe.
Description: New York : Kane Press, [2019] | Series: Bright Owl books |
Summary: Beetle does not want to share the last three leaves on the tree with Weevil and Flea, but feels bad when he sits down to eat them alone.
Identifiers: LCCN 2018024732 (print) | LCCN 2018030518 (ebook) | ISBN 9781635921052 (ebook) | ISBN 9781635921045 (pbk) | ISBN 9781635921038 (reinforced library binding)
Subjects: | CYAC: Greed—Fiction. | Beetles—Fiction. | Fleas—Fiction.
Classification: LCC PZ7.C839424 (ebook) | LCC PZ7.C839424 Gt 2019 (print) | DDC [E]—dc23
LC record available at https://lccn.loc.gov/2018024732

10 9 8 7 6 5 4 3 2 1

First published in the United States of America in 2019 by Kane Press, Inc.
Printed in China

Book Design: Michelle Martinez

Bright Owl Books is a registered trademark of Kane Press, Inc.

Visit us online at www.kanepress.com

f   Like us on Facebook
    facebook.com/kanepress

t   Follow us on Twitter
    @KanePress

GREEDY BEETLE

by Molly Coxe

Kane Press • New York

Beetle, Weevil, and Flea
live in the trees.

They eat green leaves.
They sleep.
They read.
They have everything
three bugs need.

One day,
the green leaves freeze.
A breeze blows the leaves
off the trees.

All but three.
"One for Beetle,
one for Flea,
and one for me!"
says Weevil.

"Three for me!"
says Beetle.
"Don't be greedy,"
says Weevil.
"Leave!"
says Beetle.

Beetle steams the leaves.

He sees Weevil's seat.
He sees Flea's seat.
Beetle does not feel like eating.

He does not like
the way he feels.
Beetle feels . . .

greedy!

Beetle leaps from the tree.
Weevil? Flea?
Where can they be?

22

Beetle sees Flea.

Weevil sees Beetle.
"Flee, Flea!"
she says.
"Beetle is here
to steal our green bean!"

"Don't leave!" says Beetle.
"I was greedy and mean.
I will not steal
your green bean."

"Really?" asks Flea.
"Really!" says Beetle.

Beetle, Weevil, and Flea
eat a feast for three.

They are as happy
as three bugs
can be.
"Yippee!"
says Flea.

Story Starters

It is Halloween.
What will Flea be?

Little Dear
has big ears.
What does
Little Dear hear?